If there is a keyhole to look through or a letter-box to listen at you'll find Mr Nosey there looking or listening, and probably both.

One day while Mr Nosey was taking a walk through the wood on the other side of Tiddletown he heard a door shut.

"That's odd," he said to himself.

Mr Nosey peered around a tree and there was a wall. A wall that he had never noticed before.

Now, Mr Nosey can't go past a wall without knowing what is on the other side.

And rather handily this wall had a door in it. A small yellow door.

Mr Nosey, being the nosey fellow he is, could not resist taking a look.

He opened the door and peered around it.

On the other side of the wall was a tiny house with a yellow door.

Inside the house was a lift.

Mr Nosey got in the lift and pressed the button.

The lift went down.

And down.

And down.

And down, for what seemed like a very long time.

At the bottom the lift doors opened onto a long tunnel with a light at the end.

Mr Nosey set off down the tunnel.

By this time Mr Nosey was very curious. He couldn't wait to see where the tunnel would lead.

At the end of the tunnel there was another small yellow door.

And then another tunnel.

"There must be something really interesting at the end," Mr Nosey said to himself, as he hurried along.

He came to another door and then a long,
winding staircase and another tunnel at the top.

Mr Nosey had quite lost track of time but he felt sure that he was coming close to the end.

He finally came to yet another small, yellow door just like all the others ... except this one had a keyhole.

Mr Nosey peeked through the keyhole.

All he could see was a white room. So he opened the door and there was a white room.

Nothing else!

No furniture.

No carpets.

No pictures.

Just a white room.

Mr Nosey walked into the room.

He had never been so disappointed in all his life.

He turned to leave and it was then that he saw a note stuck to the back of the door.

And written on the note was:

TEE! HEE!

SIGNED: Mr Mischief.

Mr Nosey groaned.

And went home ... the long way.

And now you know what to do if you ever discover a small, yellow door.

Keep walking!

3 Great Offers for MR.MEN Fans!

MR.MEN TOKEN

1 New Mr. Men or Little Miss Library Bus Presentation Cases

A brand new stronger, roomier school bus library box, with sturdy carrying handle and stay-closed fasteners.
The full colour, wipe-clean boxes make a great home for your full collection.
They're just £5.99 inc P&P and free bookmark!

☐ MR. MEN ☐ LITTLE MISS (please tick and order overleaf)

2 Door Hangers and Posters

In every Mr. Men and Little Miss book like this one, you will find a special token. Collect 6 tokens and we will send you a brilliant Mr. Men or Little Miss poster and a Mr. Men or Little Miss double sided full colour bedroom door hanger of your choice. Simply tick your choice in the list and tape a 50p coin for your two items to this page.

PLEASE STICK YOUR 50P COIN HERE

Door Hangers (please tick)
☐ Mr. Nosey & Mr. Muddle
☐ Mr. Slow & Mr. Busy
☐ Mr. Messy & Mr. Quiet
☐ Mr. Perfect & Mr. Forgetful
☐ Little Miss Fun & Little Miss Late
☐ Little Miss Helpful & Little Miss Tidy
☐ Little Miss Busy & Little Miss Brainy
☐ Little Miss Star & Little Miss Fun

Posters (please tick)
☐ MR.MEN
☐ LITTLE MISS

3 Sixteen Beautiful Fridge Magnets – any 2 for £2.00! inc.P&P

They're very special collector's items!
Simply tick your first and second* choices from the list below
of any 2 characters!

1st Choice

☐ Mr. Happy
☐ Mr. Lazy
☐ Mr. Topsy-Turvy
☐ Mr. Bounce
☐ Mr. Bump
☐ Mr. Small
☐ Mr. Snow
☐ Mr. Wrong

☐ Mr. Daydream
☐ Mr. Tickle
☐ Mr. Greedy
☐ Mr. Funny
☐ Little Miss Giggles
☐ Little Miss Splendid
☐ Little Miss Naughty
☐ Little Miss Sunshine

2nd Choice

☐ Mr. Happy
☐ Mr. Lazy
☐ Mr. Topsy-Turvy
☐ Mr. Bounce
☐ Mr. Bump
☐ Mr. Small
☐ Mr. Snow
☐ Mr. Wrong

☐ Mr. Daydream
☐ Mr. Tickle
☐ Mr. Greedy
☐ Mr. Funny
☐ Little Miss Giggles
☐ Little Miss Splendid
☐ Little Miss Naughty
☐ Little Miss Sunshine

*Only in case your first choice is out of stock.

TO BE COMPLETED BY AN ADULT

To apply for any of these great offers, ask an adult to complete the coupon below and send it with the appropriate payment and tokens, if needed, to MR. MEN OFFERS, PO BOX 7, MANCHESTER M19 2HD

☐ Please send _____ Mr. Men Library case(s) and/or _____ Little Miss Library case(s) at £5.99 each inc P&P

☐ Please send a poster and door hanger as selected overleaf. I enclose six tokens plus a 50p coin for P&P

☐ Please send me _____ pair(s) of Mr. Men/Little Miss fridge magnets, as selected above at £2.00 inc P&P

Fan's Name _____

Address _____

_____ **Postcode** _____

Date of Birth _____

Name of Parent/Guardian _____

Total amount enclosed £ _____

☐ **I enclose a cheque/postal order payable to Egmont Books Limited**

☐ **Please charge my MasterCard/Visa/Amex/Switch or Delta account** (delete as appropriate)

Card Number

Expiry date ___/___ **Signature** _____

Please allow 28 days for delivery. We reserve the right to change the terms of this offer at any time but we offer a 14 day money back guarantee. This does not affect your statutory rights.

MR.MEN LITTLE MISS
Mr. Men and Little Miss™ & ©Mrs. Roger Hargreaves